Music of Their Hooves

Poems About Horses

by Nancy Springer
Illustrated by Sandy Rabinowitz

WORDSONG
BOYDS MILLS PRESS

To Duchess and Danny Boy and Raider and Sheba and Finesse
and Magic Dragon and Red and Lucky and Melody. . . . — N.S.

To my children, Emily, Eric, and Toni,
and the babysitters who enabled
me to work on this book. — S.R.

Text copyright © 1994 by Nancy Springer
Illustrations copyright © 1994 by Sandy Rabinowitz

Published by Wordsong
Boyds Mills Press, Inc.
A Highlights Company
815 Church Street
Honesdale, Pennsylvania 18431
Printed in Mexico

Publisher Cataloging-in-Publication Data
Springer, Nancy.
        Music of their hooves : poems about horses / by Nancy Springer ;
illustrated by Sandy Rabinowitz.— 1st ed.
[32]p. : col. ill. ; cm.
Includes index.
Summary : Poems about horses and how their owners feel
when they ride these animals.
ISBN 1-56397-182-8
1. Horses — Juvenile poetry. 2. Children's poetry, American.
[1. Horses — Poetry.]
I. Rabinowitz, Sandy, ill. II. Title.
811.54 — dc20   1994
Library of Congress Catalog Card Number 92-84120 / AC   CIP

First edition, 1994
Book designed by Leslie Bauman
The text of this book is set in 12-point Hiroshige Book.
The illustrations are done in pencil, charcoal pencil, and watercolor.
Distributed by St. Martin's Press

10 9 8 7 6 5 4 3 2 1

Music of Their Hooves

The earth is a drum
their hooves pound the beat
the cantering cantering
rhythm of their feet

My heart is a drum
every beat of it loves
the galloping galloping
music of their hooves

4

Where We Ride To

There's a place
my horse takes me
it looks like a clover field
but really it's a mindscape
where thoughts soar like redtail hawks
circling in the high sky
my horse takes me there
to see them.

There's a place
my horse takes me
it looks like a lakeside
but really it's a heartscape
where feelings fly like wild geese
calling to the far clouds
my horse takes me there
to see them.

There's a place
my horse takes me
it looks like a pine woods
but really it's a soulscape
where dreams dart like hummingbirds
between the towering trees
my horse takes me there
to see them.

The Way

The way you sway
rocked in a cradle
as the horse walks

The way the sun
rides warm on your shoulders
as they sway

The way the horse
talks back with its ears
to everything you say

The way the sound
of hooves on clay
sets you dreaming

People say, "You're back.
So what did you see
on the trail today?"

You say, "Nothing much."
It's not what you see
it's the way. It's the way.

Talking to the Horse Trainer

"You been kicked?"
  "Yep."
"Did it hurt?"
  "Yep."
"You been bitten?"
  "Yep."
"That hurt too."
  "Uh-huh."
"Been run away with?"
  "Some days."
"Take a fall?"
  "Now and then."
"Get stepped on?"
  "Once."
"More than once."
  "That's true."
"How many times?"
  "Maybe twice."
"More than that."
  "What's your point?"
"Look at me."
  "Okay, I'm looking at you. So?"
"How come you still love horses?"
  "How come I still love you?"

Victory

There she stood, the color of my fear,
this big black animal,
the one I had to get on.
People are crazy, why do they say
riding a horse is fun anyway?
It's just plain scary
when the horse is so huge.
In my head I called her Nightmare.

She carried me along a trail in the forest,
this strong black mare,
and there were deer,
whitetail deer in the woods and they didn't run away
just looked at me big-eyed. And what I felt that day
was a power so gentle
I rode too tall for fear
and I asked the horse, and she told me:
her real name was Victory.

9

Round Round

I do not care,
I do not care
when people laugh
at my round round mare.
Her name is Hey Diddle,
she is blimpy in the middle
and cushy all over
like a beanbag chair.
But I do not care,
because I never fall.
It's like riding on a
great big fuzzy beach ball
that doesn't even bounce.
So there's never a scare.
I can ride anywhere
on my round round mare.
Why should I care?
Don't you dare
make fun of me
and my round round mare.
We do not care.
We do not care.

The Horse Next Door

The horse next door has feet like Frisbees
and a sorry-dog head with eyes full of worries.
The horse next door is a big teddy bear.
Look up and he's there with his nose in your hair.

I've thought of horses shining in the sun,
handsome, with manes flying as they run.
I've dreamed of horses with dancing feet,
the kind of horse a girl likes to meet.

And what have I got? A big clumsy pet
who wants his mommy, who's scared of the vet.
But that's okay. I know the score.
I'm in love with the horse next door.

11

The Gray Mare's Secret

The dun takes his time at the water trough,
The next one in line is the bay,
The brown horse lays back his ears as he drinks,
And the very last horse is the gray.

The dun kicks the bay horse, the bay bites the brown
And drives him away from his hay,
The brown horse can't kick the bay or the dun,
But they all can kick the gray.

Three horses graze on the sunny hilltop,
The dun and the brown and the bay.
One horse grazes alone in the valley,
A little mare, dapple gray.

They remind me of three school bullies
Who don't want the new kid to play.
I wish they would let the gray mare join them,
But that's not the horse herd way.

The gray mare carries a secret inside her.
Maybe she knows that someday
Her foal will grow up to run beside her,
And play, and graze, and be gray.

The New Mustang

You are shaggy and ribby and small,
little horse,
but your hooves make thunder
big as the sky you were born under

      out there in Nevada
      with seven storms brewing
      on the far horizon all at once—
      I will call you Seven Storms.

They forced you into the corral,
little mustang,
and into the chute, and into the vetting ring
but I will not force you into anything

      no need to run like lightning
      to the far end of the pen
      and snort at me with wild fire in your eyes—
      I will call you Lightning Wildfire.

They brought you to Pennsylvania
of all places
and it must seem very strange to you here
with the hills so small and dark and near

      and the pink mist in the narrow sky
      and the trees so tall you shy in fear
      you stare with ears fox-pricked in wonder—
      I will call you Nevada Fox.

You do not know how good oats are,
wild mustang,
or brushing, but soon I will show you
and you will be brave and shining new

> but you are shining now, little one,
> with your wide eyes looking for the sun,
> and I love you
> someday you will love me too—
> I will call you Son of Thunder
> I will call you Beloved.

The Wild Stallion

He does not shine
scars do not shine in the sun
and he carries many scars

> from the hard hind feet of mares
> from the hard teeth of rivals
> from the hard land itself

his mane and tail torn short by sagebrush
his hooves worn down by stones

he does not shine
he does not wear the scars like medals

> glory does not find water
> glory does not find grass
> glory does not save foals from coyotes

he does not care about scars at all
and when he stands on the mesa
to sample the air for the smell of danger
it is not so you can call him beautiful

The Appaloosa

The sorrel horse of sunset
And the silver horse of dawn,
Neither of them is mine.
The black horse of the north wind,
The blood bay of the south,
Neither of them is mine.

The stallion of the high sky
And the great brown mare of earth,
Neither of them is mine;
But the spotted horse with wild white eyes,
Him I ride until we fly,
Until we fly.

The Wish Horse

Look down there
in the dusk by the river
there's a hope loose in the hollow tonight

The wish horse
walks white in the valley
hush white, whisper white in the twilight

No rider
no saddle and no bridle
just a glimmer the color of moonlight

Then you see
a mane like mist rising
eyes stardeep as a lake at midnight

Just once
you see it light the shadows
then it's gone like an angel, out of sight

Just once
and never again it walks for you
when you blink it's lost in the night

So wish
when it lifts its head wish quickly
wish for love, life, happiness, light

Whatever happens
you are lucky
because once in a twilight
you saw the moon white pearl bright

Wish horse

Thank You Stormy

Dear Stormy Lady,

My horse I'm writing you
to thank you for taking me
up the wildflower trail
where the air smelled like angels

and getting me around the fallen tree
and being calm when the grapevine
grabbed you under the belly
and backing up when I asked you to
even though you don't like to do it

Thank you for bringing me home
when I got us kind of lost
up there on the mountain
and thank you for standing still
as a tree trunk when we met up with
the skunk

I promise I will bring you
wild pears like the deer eat
and shampoo your mane and tail
and never let your water go dry
again

I am not a perfect human
You are not a perfect horse
But today we were a team
Thank you Stormy
I love you

Forever,

Lisa

Summer

His mane shines almost purple in the sun
I go to him down the hazy pasture
In summer he smells like butter
Larks sing throaty in the long grass

I go to him down the hazy pasture
He lifts his head from his grazing
Larks sing throaty in the long grass
Horses move slowly in the heat

He lifts his head from his grazing
Today he will not run from me
Horses move slowly in the heat
The sun hangs heavy like an egg yolk

Today he will not run from me
I walk up to him and give him sugar
The sun hangs heavy like an egg yolk
The smell of yellow flowers oils the air

I walk up to him and give him sugar
I talk to him and slip the halter on
The smell of yellow flowers oils the air
I smooth the mane away from his hot ears

I talk to him and slip the halter on
In summer he smells like butter
I smooth the mane away from his hot ears
His mane shines almost purple in the sun

That Morning

He was born
on a winter morning
with a red star in the eastern sky
and a pure white star between his eyes
he was shaking and wet and weak
he could barely stand on his feet
I cradled him and helped him eat
that morning

Now see him run
in the summer sun
racing the redbirds in the sky
running in the white clover, flying by
His legs are straight and slim and long
his back is short and shining and strong
I knew he would be fine all along
He's the one

Some dawn
next summer I'll get on
One red star will shine in the sky
one white flash of fear will shine in his eyes
but I will ride him gently
and he will know he can trust me
because I have loved him since the morning
he was born

She Loved to Run

Her forefeet were so sore
toward the end she couldn't run anymore
and the blue fire went out of her eyes.

Now when I see the sunrise
I see my mare running on silver.

Now when I see the sunset
I see my mare running on gold.

Now when I see the deep sky
I see her deep eyes on fire with running.

I miss her
but it's better this way.
Her name was Looking To The Sun,
and she loved to run.

What Scares My Mare

Usually what it takes to make
her rear up and hit the sky
is one good look at a snake,
but today I rode her right by one—
and so I relaxed, which was a mistake,
because just then a yellow butterfly
        lit right on her eye,
        she blew sky-high,
and I did a flip like a pancake—
so about this cast on my arm, that's why.
Not because of a big black snake,
just a little
            yellow
                attack
                    butterfly.

28

To Gentle Him

He kicked me
in the thigh
so hard
his hoof left a bruise
big as a plate
black as him
and it hurt
so bad
I had to cry
and I
thought it was broken
and I thought I'd never
go near him again.

Nothing was broken
and then I wanted to
punish him
and hit him with the whip
but I went
and looked into his eyes
instead
and then
I saw how scared he was
because so was I
so I put the whip away
and left my fear with it
and began
all over
again

29

Since Prince

Before my horse came
I was a loner
I wore old clothes
I watched for rainbows
I was a dreamer
They said I needed help.

His name is Prince
He's a blood red bay
a Thoroughbred
with a golden bugle neigh
When we're happy we dance
He prances me around.

Now I ride every day.
I am a dreamer
I wear old clothes
I watch for rainbows
I need help, they say.
But Prince made a difference
That they don't see.
Now I'm proud to be me.

Horse

High tail
Over the hilltop
Running to the sky
Sunlight in your flying mane
Ever free

Index of Titles and First Lines